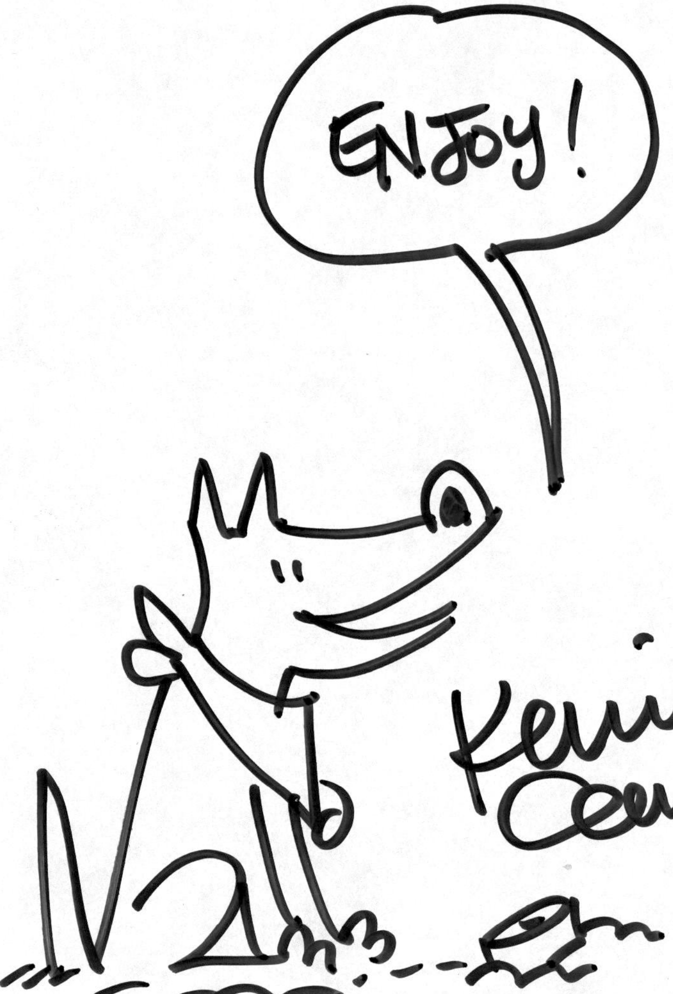

Kevin
2010

To the Shanedling Family,
Happy Skating!
Andrew

THANK YOU TO OUR FAMILIES FOR THEIR
ENCOURAGEMENT, AND TO MOLLY BACKES,
SCOTT SAMUELSON AND ZANDER CANNON
FOR THEIR CONTRIBUTIONS!

FOR BEN, LUCY AND ALL
THE FUTURE RINK RATS
-A.S. & T.H.

FOR RUBY
-K.C.

ISBN 10: 1-59298-362-6
ISBN 13: 978-1-59298-362-9

Library of Congress Catalog Number: 2010938658

Printed in the United States of America

First Printing: 2010

15   14   13   12   11   5   4   3   2   1

Cover and interior design by Kevin Cannon

Good Sport Books
www.GoodSportBooks.com

Beaver's Pond Press, Inc.
7104 Ohms Lane, Suite 101
Edina, MN 55439-2129
(952) 829-8818
www.BeaversPondPress.com

BEAVER'S
POND
PRESS

To order, visit
www.BookHouseFulfillment.com
www.BeaversPondBooks.com
or call 1-800-901-3480

Reseller discounts available.

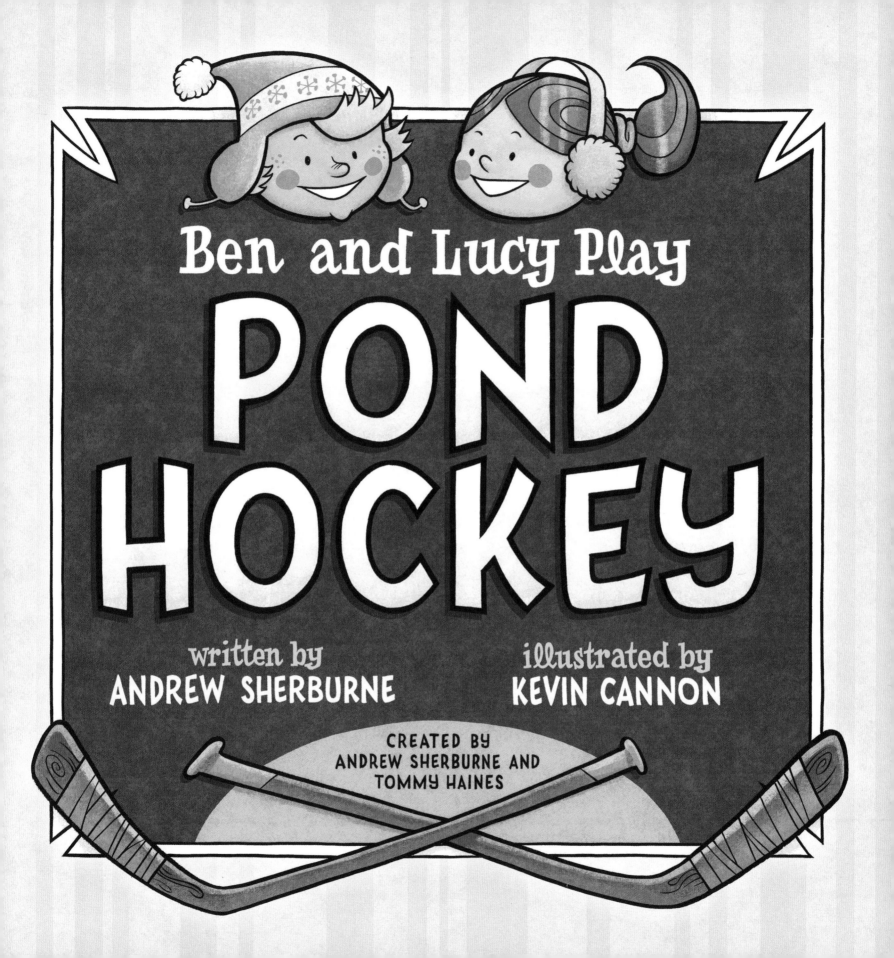

Ben and Lucy Play

POND HOCKEY

written by
ANDREW SHERBURNE

illustrated by
KEVIN CANNON

CREATED BY
ANDREW SHERBURNE AND
TOMMY HAINES

The WINTER SUN RISES to WELCOME the DAY,

The POND'S finally FROZEN and READY for PLAY.

Ben

Lucy

BEN and LUCY BUNDLE UP and, READY to GO, put STICKS on their SHOULDERS to TREK through the SNOW.

They RUSH
to the RINK in
the BRISK winter AIR,

KNOWING that their
FRIENDS will ALSO
be THERE.

Ben **SITS**
in the **SNOWBANK**,
NEXT to the **LAKE**,

And **TUGS** on his **LACES**
to **TIGHTEN** his
SKATES.

While **BEN**, with his **BOOTS**, marks off the **GOAL**.

Lucy
KNEELS on the ICE
and COVERS her EYES,

SHUFFLING STICKS from
the MIDDLE to CHOOSE
up the SIDES.

BEN and
LUCY line up to
SKATE with the WIND...

...TAKE the ICE!

Lucy ZIG-ZAGS and ZOOMS, then FLIPS IT to BEN,

Who DANGLES and DEKES and PASSES AGAIN.

They SPEED down the ICE through the BLUSTERY COLD,

PASSING and TWIRLING, then SHOOTING...

They **SMILE** and they **LAUGH**, they **SCREAM** and they **SHOUT**,

They **SKATE** all day **LONG**, but **NEVER** tire **OUT**.

What FUN
BEN and LUCY
have HAD at the PARK,

Now it's TIME to go HOME,
the SKY'S getting
DARK.

Hot **COCOA**
AWAITS them, all
THANKS to **MOM,**

A **PERFECT**
warm ending...

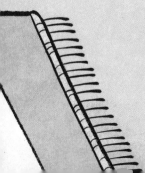

...to a DAY at the POND.